Rollerblade Crusade

Suzanne Weyn

PRICE STERN SLOAN
Los Angeles

For Carolan Suzanne Weyn

Published by Price Stern Sloan, Inc.
11150 Olympic Boulevard
Los Angeles, California 90064
ISBN: 0-8431-3413-5
Printed in the United States of America
10 9 8 7 6 5 4 3 2

Contents

Sun and Fun

Barbie threw her suitcase down on the bed. "Wow!" she cried. "This place is great!"

"It's even better than I hoped it would be," agreed her friend Christie.

Barbie and Christie were on vacation. Barbie's cousin owned the large fancy hotel where they were staying. It was right on the beach. He'd told them to stay as long as they wanted.

The two-room suite had an open porch that faced the ocean. Barbie went out onto the porch and let the ocean breeze ruffle her long blond hair. Christie joined her. "That water looks great!" Barbie said. "I can't wait for the rest of the gang to get here."

Their friends had all taken rooms at the hotel. Steve and Ken were in the room below them. Kira and Teresa were down the hall.

Christie pulled her thick black hair back with a yellow bow. "I don't know what to do first," she said. "Should I swim? Or should I hit the walk with my Rollerblade® in-line skates?"

"I brought my skates too," Barbie said.

"Let's skate, then," Christie decided.

They went back inside and began to unpack. After a while, a voice came from the hall. "Hey, guys!" It was Kira.

"We're in here," Barbie called.

Kira came in and bounced onto one of the beds. Her black hair flew up behind her. "This is going to be the best summer ever!" she cried.

Christie smiled. "I guess you're a little excited," she said.

"I never saw such excitement," said Teresa. She stood in the doorway, her green eyes amused.

"Why shouldn't I be?" asked Kira. "This place has it all—a beach, cute little places to eat, a park and a great cement walk for trying out my new Rollerblade® in-line skates!"

"You should have seen her out there admiring the cement," Teresa said with a chuckle.

"It's the best," said Kira. "It's new and smooth. Not a single crack. Just right for skating."

"We were just deciding whether to go swimming or skating first," said Barbie.

"I vote for skating," said Kira.

"I know why you want to skate," Teresa teased Kira. "On the way in we saw a very cute guy doing some awesome skating."

Kira shrugged. "I wouldn't mind skating past him. Maybe he's my Prince Charming, only he's wearing Rollerblade® in-line skates instead of a crown."

"You have some imagination," said Christie.

"You never know," said Kira.

Barbie pulled a pair of pink-and-white elbow and knee pads from her suitcase. "How do you like my new protective gear? Since the pads are as important as the skates, I bought some to match!" she said.

"They're hot!" Christie told her.

"Come on, Teresa," said Kira, getting off the bed. "Let's go back to our room and get our skates and pads and stuff." She turned to Barbie and Christie. "We'll meet you in the lobby in ten minutes."

Barbie strapped her purple purse pack around the waist of her white bike shorts with pink trim. Christie changed into a purple leotard with yellow bicycle shorts. "Let's go," she said.

They met up with Kira and Teresa in the lobby and hurried onto the walk. People in swimsuits went back and forth from the ocean to the small food booths that lined the curbs. Quite a few skaters whizzed past them.

They sat on a park bench and laced up their skates. Christie spun out onto the walk making wide circles. Kira—dressed in a pair of shiny blue bike shorts and a blue-and-yellow halter top—was the next one up. She skated out, lifting her back leg.

Barbie joined them. She skated backward in a curving line.

The last one up was Teresa. "I'm still a little shaky on these," she told Barbie. Slowly, she wobbled over to her friends.

Kira and Christie skated to Teresa. "Here you go," they said.

"Whoa!" cried Teresa, laughing as her feet flew wide apart.

Barbie caught her. "It's a different way of balancing than on regular roller skates," she told Teresa. "Once you get the hang of it, you'll be fine."

It didn't take long for Teresa to catch on. Pretty soon she stopped shaking and began to really skate.

"Don't look now," Teresa said, skating past Kira, "but that cute guy we saw is skating our way."

2

Mitch

"Hello, ladies," the handsome young man greeted them. He had light blue eyes, a deep tan and lots of muscles. His light brown hair was combed straight back and tied in a ponytail. He wore a gray vest over a white tank shirt, orange-and-gray pants and some funky beads. He spun twice on his skates. "What's happening?"

"We're working on our skating moves," said Kira, smiling at him.

"I could show you some cool stuff," Mitch said. He skated backward, then tipped forward on his skates and began to spin. Slowly he bent one knee up so that he was spinning on one skate.

"Amazing!" Teresa cried.

"The guy is good," Christie agreed. "Very good."

In a moment, Mitch stopped spinning.

"Can you do this?" Christie asked. She skated until she was going very fast. Then she crouched so that she was sitting. Her right leg shot out, and she started to spin. Still spinning, she rose to a standing position.

"Not bad," the young man admitted. "I may have met my match. My name is Mitch."

Barbie smiled. "I'm Barbie, and these are my friends Kira and Teresa. Our superskater is Christie."

"Nice to meet you. Hey, Christie, I've got one for you," Mitch said. He got up some speed and then flew off the ground into a forward flip. He skated toward them and bowed deeply as they clapped.

Christie laughed. "You've got me beat in the flips," she said. "I try to keep at least one skate on the ground at all times."

"You're pretty good, though," Mitch told her. "How about the rest of you ladies? Know any skating tricks?"

"I'm just learning," said Teresa.

"I'd love to learn some tricks," Kira said, skating around Mitch.

"I'll show you some," said Christie. Kira skated behind Mitch and made a face at Christie. "Oh, but of course Mitch could show you better than I could," Christie added quickly. Still behind Mitch, Kira smiled at Christie.

"I'd be glad to show you all," said Mitch. "Hey, you know what? If you ladies are serious, you should enter the contest down at Marv's Pizza Parlor."

"What is that?" asked Barbie.

"It's a Rollerblade® in-line skate contest that Marv has each week. He has it in front of his place on the walk. Lots of people come to see it. The contest brings him a ton of business and it's a lot of fun to watch. You could enter the group-skating category. But don't bother with the singles category. I'm the reigning champ. I win every week."

"Modest, aren't you?" Christie teased.

"Hey, the truth is the truth," Mitch replied. "I'm the best around here."

"He's certainly the best looking," Kira whispered to Barbie as she skated up behind her.

"He _is_ cute," Barbie whispered back.

"What's the prize for winning this contest?" Christie asked.

"A free pizza party for you and ten of your best friends. Marv gives you all you can eat and drink. Maybe I'll invite you gals next week when I win."

"Maybe we'll invite you when _we_ win," said Kira.

"Cool," Mitch said.

Barbie looked at her friends. "What do you say? Want to try for it?"

"You all should try. I'll just hold you back," Teresa said.

"Don't be silly. Either you join us, or we're

not doing it," said Barbie.

"Then I guess I have to," said Teresa, smiling. "But I'll need lots of help!" she added.

"No problem," Barbie said. "What are friends for?"

"The contest is every Friday night. Since it's Saturday, you just missed the last one," Mitch told them. "You should skate down there now and sign up. Marv takes only five entries in each category. The list fills up pretty fast."

"Let's go for it," Christie said. "Thanks for the tip, Mitch."

"Sure thing," said Mitch. "I'm always hanging out on the walk. If you need any help or pointers, don't be shy, just give a holler."

"Oh, we won't," said Kira. "I'm sure we'll need lots of help."

"No problem," said Mitch as he skated away.

"Oh, I'm sure we'll need lots of help," Christie teased Kira when he was gone.

"You can't blame me for trying," Kira said,

giggling. "He's so adorable."

Barbie pushed off on her skates. "Let's skate down the walk and go find Marv," she said.

"I'm with you," said Christie, skating behind her. "There's no sense wasting time."

"That's right," Barbie agreed. "We have a lot of rehearsing to do."

3

An Unpleasant Surprise

"Are you guys going to skate until midnight?" asked Ken. He had come up to the walk from the beach. He was dressed in pink-and-blue checked swimming trunks and carried a green tape player.

"Yeah, this is turning into one lonely vacation for Ken and me," added Steve, who was dressed in orange-and-yellow trunks.

It was late in the afternoon the next day. Barbie, Kira, Teresa and Christie had spent all of it working on their skating routine.

"Hey, let's see that tape player," said Christie, skating up to Ken. "It's just what we need to add music to our routine."

"You're welcome to it," said Ken. "But take a break, huh? You guys have been working all day."

"Sorry," said Christie. "I guess we lost track of time."

"Christie is whipping me into shape for the big contest," Teresa added.

"She's doing great, too," Christie told the guys. "She's going to be better than all of us."

"Well, stop rolling and come eat," said Ken. "Steve and I made a barbecue down on the beach."

"Food!" cried Kira. "I can't think of anything I'd rather have right now than a burger and a soda!"

"Except maybe a date with Mitch," Teresa said.

"Wasn't that nice of him to come help us today?" said Kira, skating in a circle. "With his help we could win!"

"This guy probably just wants to hang around with a bunch of pretty girls," said Steve. "I don't know if I like that."

"Don't worry about me," said Christie. "I'm

sticking with you. Besides, Kira has already called dibs on Mitch. She likes him."

"But does he like me?" Kira asked glumly. "So far, he just seems to like all of us."

"Give it time," said Barbie, taking Ken's hand.

The friends took off their skates and hurried down to the beach. "Do you believe we haven't even been swimming yet?" cried Kira. "I'm going to jump right in."

She peeled off her T-shirt and shorts. Underneath she wore a neon green one-piece swimsuit with a wild, colorful pattern. She began to run toward the water.

"Wait for me!" cried Christie, pulling off her blue midriff top and jean shorts.

Barbie, Teresa, Ken and Steve settled in on a blanket near a low grill. "Smell those hamburgers," said Teresa hungrily.

"They'll be done in a minute," said Steve. "Do you really think you have a chance to win this contest?"

"I think we're getting good," said Teresa. "We did basic moves today. Tomorrow we'll start making up our routine. Now we need a name for our group, and we need a song to skate to."

"How about the Good Skates?" said Ken.

"I don't think so," Teresa said, wrinkling her nose.

"What about the Wild Wheels?" Steve said as he put a burger on a bun and handed it to Barbie.

"We're not really wild," Barbie said.

"I know," said Ken. "The Rockin' Rollers."

"I kind of like that," Barbie said.

"So do I," said Teresa.

Just then Kira and Christie returned from their swim. Ken tossed them each a towel. Steve handed them hamburgers.

"The water is great," said Kira.

The gang ate, swam and laughed on the beach for two more hours. "Anyone want to build a sand castle?" Barbie asked.

Everyone did. They got up and walked to the water's edge. Soon they were building tunnels, walls and towers. Teresa let the wet sand drip through her fingers, making lovely, drippy designs on the castle walls.

When it was done, they stood back and admired it. "It's beautiful," said Christie.

"The sad thing about sand castles is that the tide always comes in and washes them away," Kira added.

They decided to walk along the water. The sun was just beginning to set, throwing a slightly pink haze over everything. "The tide is starting to turn now," noted Barbie after a while. "I wonder how our castle is doing."

On their way back, they stopped to check on the castle. "Yuck!" cried Kira when she got to it. "What is this stuff?"

The others joined her. The tide had reached the front wall, and the sand was covered with wet plastic bags, rubber gloves and all sorts of garbage.

"Oh, how horrible!" said Christie. "All that junk is floating in the surf."

"It's being washed in with the tide," said Ken. "Somebody dumped it into the ocean. Who would do such a thing?"

"I wish we knew," said Barbie.

4

Whale Watch

The next morning the gang stood on a dock. They had decided to go on a whale-watching tour. The air was a little cool. Barbie was glad she had worn her jean jacket with the red-white-and-blue trim.

Soon a short, stocky man in a captain's hat came onto the dock. "Step aboard," he said, helping the group onto his midsize cruise ship.

The captain started the boat. "We saw two humpbacks yesterday. There's a good chance they're not far away today."

The boat traveled out into the ocean. Barbie sat near the side and smelled the crisp salt breeze. She shut her blue eyes and let the sun shine down on her.

"What are you thinking?" Ken asked.

"I was thinking about that garbage on the

beach," she told him. "How could someone dump it into the sea?"

"It's greed," said Ken. "Private companies have to pay to have their garbage taken away. It's cheaper to dump it than to get rid of it properly."

"But don't they know we all share the ocean? If they ruin it, there's no getting it back. Not to mention all the creatures that live in the ocean."

"I guess whoever is doing it simply doesn't care," Ken said sadly.

Just then, the captain cut the engine. "Look to your right, everybody," he said. The gang crowded to the side of the boat. Just then a huge, shiny black back rose out of the water, churning the sea around it. "Thar she blows!" shouted the captain. The whale shot a stream of water from the blowhole at the top of its head.

"Here comes another one!" said Teresa. A

second black back appeared beside the first, also sending up a stream of water.

"I'm guessing this is a male and female couple," the captain told them.

The whales didn't seem to care that the boat was nearby. They swam together, coming to the surface often.

After a few moments, the captain slowed the boat. He leaned over the side and sighed deeply. "What's wrong?" Barbie asked him.

"It's another floating patch of garbage," the captain said. "We've been seeing a whole lot of it lately. Last week a whale beached itself not far from here. The coast guard and some marine biologists tried to help it, but they couldn't get the big guy to turn around and swim out to sea."

"Do they know why?" Barbie asked.

"They're not sure, but they think it has to do with pollution. The whales' sonar gets messed up when there's a lot of junk in the ocean."

"That's awful," said Barbie.

"It sure is," agreed the captain. "Hey, I didn't mean to ruin your trip with bad news. Go look at the whales."

Barbie went back to her whale watching. But now her mind wasn't on it. She kept thinking about the dumping. Something had to be done about it.

An hour later, when the boat returned to the dock, the gang got off and went to have some lunch. They found a lovely outdoor restaurant right on the beach. "Why isn't anyone doing anything about this?" asked Barbie as she picked at her fried clams.

"Uh-oh," said Christie. "I've seen that look in your eyes before. What have you got in mind?"

"Why don't we take a trip into town and talk to the mayor," Barbie said. "Maybe no one has told him or her that this is going on."

"It wouldn't hurt to try," said Ken.

After lunch, the gang piled into Barbie's pink

1957 Chevy and drove into town. The mayor's office was at the end of a neat town park.

They waited a half hour before getting in to see Mayor Hanover. Barbie told the tall, thin man what they'd seen. "Can't you do anything to stop it?" she asked.

"I'm glad you came to me because I was not aware of this," he told her. "It must have just started happening. You know, of course, that this is a crime. No one is allowed to dump in the ocean around here."

"Then why don't you just arrest whoever is doing it?" asked Teresa.

"We have to find out who it is first," the mayor replied. "We have a very small police force. This is a peaceful town."

"Could you get outside help?" Barbie pressed.

"I can try, but it will take a little while," the mayor told her. "There's paperwork to be done. And then an inspector needs to come and prove that there really is a problem."

"There's a problem, all right," said Christie.

"I'll do my best," said the mayor.

"He's going to take forever to do anything," said Christie when they were outside.

"I know," said Barbie, thinking. "Maybe we are going to have to speed things up a bit."

5

Kira Makes Her Move

"Look at him," Kira sighed later that afternoon. "Isn't he cute?" Mitch was the center of attention. A crowd had gathered on the walk to watch his skating.

"You've really got a crush on him," said Barbie at her side.

"Why doesn't he ask me out?" Kira asked, frowning. "I don't see him with a girlfriend. He must get the idea by now that I like him."

"Maybe he feels shy about it. After all, the rest of us are always around."

Kira's dark eyes lit happily. "That's got to be it!" she cried. "Of course! You're a genius!" Then she knit her brows. "But how will I get to talk to him alone?"

Barbie thought. "You might—"

"I know!" Kira cried, cutting her off. "I

brought my camera with me. I'll tell him I want to get pictures of him skating for a photo project I'm working on."

"Since you really are a photographer, I suppose that would work," Barbie agreed.

"Ready for practice?" asked Christie, skating up to them along with Teresa.

"Sure," said Barbie.

"Can I be excused for now?" Kira asked. "I want to get to know Mitch better."

"Kira!" Christie said sternly. "How will we ever get this thing going if—"

"Come on, Christie," said Teresa. "This is a vacation, not a Rollerblade® in-line skate training camp."

"Oh, all right," Christie huffed.

"Let's get started," said Barbie.

Barbie skated off with Christie and Teresa. As she skated, she kept one eye on Kira. She was curious to see how she would do with Mitch.

When Mitch finished his act, the crowd around him left. That's when Kira approached. Barbie saw Kira pointing at her camera. Mitch nodded and smiled. So far so good, thought Barbie.

Kira began snapping pictures of Mitch doing his different tricks. Mitch seemed happy to show her his entire routine. When they were done, they sat on a bench.

"How's she doing?" Christie asked, skating near Barbie.

"They're talking, anyway," said Barbie.

"Do you like him?" Christie asked.

"He's OK," Barbie answered.

"Oh, Barbie, you always think the best of people," Christie scoffed. "I don't know. There's something about him. He's a big show-off."

Teresa skated up to them. "How's Kira doing on Mitch patrol?" she asked.

"She's about to tell us herself," said Barbie. With her skates slung over her shoulder, Kira walked toward them. She didn't look happy.

"What's the matter?" Barbie asked when Kira arrived.

Kira groaned. "I feel so silly! Things were going so well that I got up my nerve and asked him to go to the movies with me some night."

"Good for you," said Barbie.

"It might have been good if he had said yes, but he said no!" Kira blurted.

"I don't believe it!" cried Christie.

"He said he works nights. Every night! If that's not a brush-off, what is?"

"Maybe he really does work," said Teresa. "That would explain why he's around all afternoon."

"He would just get in the way of our skating," said Christie.

"Besides," Barbie added. "We're going to be busy tonight. Don't you remember?"

"I didn't forget, Barbie," said Kira. "But I think it's going to be a waste of time." The gang was going to camp out on the beach that night. The plan was to watch for the dumpers.

"They've got to be dumping nearby," Barbie said. "There would be less stuff washing up if they were far away. Maybe we'll see something. Maybe we won't. But it's a place to start."

"I'll be there," said Kira. "It's not like I have a date or anything."

That night at about eleven, the gang gathered on the beach. They built a fire and sang songs. "This is like being back at camp," Barbie said.

By two in the morning, they needed to sleep. They decided to take turns keeping watch. Barbie took the first shift.

She sat, hugging her knees, watching the moonbeams dance on the waves. There in the quiet night, with only the lapping of the waves, Barbie felt the power of the ocean. How could anyone treat it with such a lack of respect?

Just then, the black figure of a small motorboat appeared way out on the ocean. Only a small green blinking light guided its way. Barbie got to her knees and grabbed the field glasses by her side. "Wake up, everybody," she said as she studied the boat.

"What...what is it?" mumbled Christie. "Do you see something?"

"I sure do," said Barbie. "Those guys are dumping big bags into the water."

6

Taking Action

Early the next morning, Barbie was out on the beach. The rest of the gang was still asleep back at the hotel. This is awful, she thought, looking down at the garbage washing in with the tide.

Behind her, workers in green uniforms cleaned the beach. They stabbed garbage with the sharp end of long poles. A small truck ran up and down the shore. At the front of it, a wide wheel turned, sifting small pieces of glass and bottle tops from the sand. The driver stopped when he reached Barbie. "Pretty disgusting, huh?" the young man said, gazing at the garbage in the surf.

"It sure is," Barbie agreed.

"We clean this beach every morning," he told her. "But we can't keep up with this new stuff. It just keeps washing in. If it's not stopped, they're going to have to close this beach."

Barbie gasped. "How terrible!"

"No kidding," said the man, pushing the brim of his cap away from his forehead. "Not only will it be a drag for vacationers, but think of all the people who will lose their jobs. Me and my staff, for starters. And it will drive those restaurants out of business, and the hotels. It'll be a disaster."

"I hadn't thought of all that," Barbie admitted.

"I think of it every morning when I see all this stuff floating around. I wish I knew who was doing this."

As he spoke, Barbie noticed a large wire net attached to his truck. "Could I borrow that?" she asked.

"Here," he said, handing the net to her. "But if you're going to try to clean it up, don't bother. One person can't do it."

"I was thinking that the garbage might give me a clue as to where it comes from," she said.

"Here, then take these, too," he said, handing her a pair of rubber gloves. "You don't want to be touching that stuff. Who knows where it came from."

"Thanks," Barbie said, taking the gloves. When he drove away, she took the net and dragged it through the water. She scooped up small bottles, eyedroppers, plastic gloves, test tubes, lipstick and mascara tubes and a broken makeup compact. She sat down on the beach and put on the gloves. Gingerly, she picked through the junk, examining each item.

"Find anything interesting?" asked Kira, sitting down beside her on the sand.

"I might have," said Barbie, turning a lipstick tube in her gloved hand. "None of this stuff has any brand name on it."

"Could it have washed off in the water?"

"Not overnight." Barbie tossed the lipstick back in the net and pulled off her gloves. "What I'm thinking is that this stuff must

come from a cosmetics lab nearby."

"What do we do next?" asked Kira. "We could show these things to the mayor, I suppose."

Barbie got to her feet. "I might have a better idea. Why don't we visit the local paper? If they print a story about this, someone might come forward with more information."

"Great idea," said Kira.

They drove downtown to the *Sun Gazette* building.

At the front desk they were directed to Sonia Lasman's office. "She has the beach beat," the woman told them.

Sonia Lasman was a short, plump woman with bright red hair and thick glasses. "How can I help you gals?" she asked when they came in.

They told her their story. When they were done, Sonia pounded her fist on a pile of papers. "I knew it!" she cried. "I've been saying it all along, but no one will listen."

"Listen to what?" asked Barbie.

"It's that Rose's Cosmetics lab right out on the end of the cove! They are the pits! They test products on animals, and they pay their workers next to nothing. They're real creeps. I've been saying they've been dumping, but I can't get the proof. And without proof, there's nothing I can do. I tried to sneak out there one night, but they have the road fenced off. I couldn't get in."

"What if we could get you some proof?" Barbie asked.

"We could nail them," Sonia said. "But how would you do that?"

"You said they're on the cove. Could someone get there by water? You know, take a boat in?"

"I guess so," said Sonia. "It might be tricky. They don't have a dock or anything."

"What are you thinking?" Kira asked Barbie.

Barbie smiled. "I think it's time for us to do a little detective work."

7

Dark Discovery

"I think that's it, over there," Barbie said, pointing. She leaned over the side of their rented motorboat. It was night and hard to see. But she'd gotten a local map and knew they were near the tip of the cove.

"I see a big building there," said Christie, peering into the darkness.

Ken turned the boat toward the cove. "Is your camera ready?" he asked Kira.

She finished loading her low-light film. Then she snapped on a long lens. "All set," she said. "This camera is great for taking night pictures. And the zoom lens will let me get close-up shots from far away."

"This is kind of exciting," whispered Teresa. "I feel like I'm in a movie."

"Except this is real," said Steve. He looked

over the side of the boat. "And there might be very sharp rocks under us. Take it slow, Ken."

As they neared the lab, Ken slowed the engine. There was a high fence around most of the building, but on the sea side it was wide open. "The dumpers are coming by boat," Barbie reminded them. "So we don't want to be sitting right here where they can see us."

"I could anchor over by those rocks," Ken said.

"Good idea, but be careful," Barbie said.

Ken dropped anchor and cut the engine. After kicking off their shoes, Barbie, Kira and Christie slid over the side of the boat. "Good thing we wore shorts," said Christie as the water lapped at her knees.

"You three stay in the boat," Barbie told Ken, Steve and Teresa. "We may have to get out of here fast if there are guards or if the dumpers spot us."

Kira put her camera strap around her neck as the three of them waded toward the rocks.

Carefully, they climbed the dark, slippery rocks. When they were crouched at the top, they had a good view of the lab's loading dock. Although a wide driveway went right to it, the ocean was also nearby.

Ten minutes later a motorboat anchored just off shore. Two strongly built men jumped off the boat and waded to shore. One was balding and the other wore a baseball cap. Otherwise, they were too far away to see clearly. "This is it," Barbie told Kira. "Start taking pictures."

Kira snapped away as the men carted bag after bag of garbage out onto their boats.

"It would be great if we could get pictures of them actually dumping the stuff," said Christie.

"You're right," Barbie agreed. "Just seeing them carrying bags of garbage doesn't really prove anything."

"Let's go get them, then," said Kira.

They climbed down the rocks. "We want to

follow them," Barbie told Ken. "We want shots of them dumping."

"OK," said Ken. He waited until the dumpers' boat had started up again, and then he turned on his engine. Just then, the moon dipped behind a cloud, and the night became pitch-dark. "I'm going to have to stay pretty close to them or I won't be able to see them," Ken said.

"Do your best," said Barbie.

The gang followed the dumpers out into the ocean. "They're stopping," Steve said after a short while.

Ken cut the engine. Holding her camera, Kira climbed onto the bow of the boat. She lay flat and focused her lens.

They heard a splash as the first bag of garbage hit the water. Barbie cringed at the sound. Then there was another splash and another. "This will be the last time they ever do this," she said.

At that moment, the full moon came out from behind the cloud. It lit the ocean. Barbie saw the two men turn toward their boat. Suddenly they shined a bright floodlight on them.

Kira quickly crawled back off the bow. "Time to get out of here," said Ken, gunning the motor. At top speed, he pulled the boat in a circle away from the dumpers.

But the men had a fast boat too. They also threw their engine into high gear and began to chase after the gang.

"What will they do if they catch us?" asked Teresa.

"They're not going to," said Ken.

"I hope you're right," said Christie, "because they're getting very close!"

Ken drove the boat in a wide zigzag path. The two men stayed with him. Barbie looked at Ken's tense face. She hoped the dumpers didn't catch up. It might be a very unpleasant scene.

At that moment, the lights of a large seaside restaurant began to flicker. "Head that way!" Barbie yelled. Ken steered the boat toward the lights. In a few minutes, he was inside its well-lit marina.

Just behind them, the dumpers slowed their engines and then turned and disappeared into the night.

Ken let the boat idle. The gang looked at one another. "Whew!" said Kira. "That was sure close."

8

The Night Job Ends

"That creep! How could he? I can't believe this!" shouted Kira, flipping through the photos in her hand. She sat in the passenger seat of Barbie's Chevy the next morning. They were parked in front of an one-hour photo lab. Kira had just gotten back the pictures of the dumpers.

"Why are you so upset?" asked Barbie. "Let me see those." Kira handed her the pictures. Barbie looked at the first one. "Oh my gosh," she said quietly.

"Let me see," said Christie, reaching forward from the backseat. She and Teresa looked at the pictures Barbie handed back.

Teresa gasped. "It's Mitch! He's one of the dumpers."

"I told you I never liked that guy," said Christie.

Kira slumped in her seat. "So that was his big night job. He wasn't lying about that. Last night I thought the guy looked familiar, but it was too dark to see."

Barbie patted Kira on the shoulder. "See, it's good that you didn't go out with him."

Kira groaned. "How could I have even liked such a monster?"

"You didn't know," said Teresa. "I never would have guessed he was the one."

"Let's go see Sonia Lasman," said Barbie, starting the car. They drove to the office and went in to see the reporter.

"You gals are awesome! Amazing!" the woman cried. She clutched the photos to her heart and did a small jig of joy around the office. "Good-bye, Rose's. Hello, clean water. After I make a few phone calls, this case will be closed. But first let me get your full names. You are all going to be in my front-page story!"

They gave their names, adding Ken's and

Steve's. "By the way," said Kira as she was about to leave, "the guy with the cap is named Mitch. You can find him skating on the walk."

"Thanks," said Sonia, making a note. "You gals are true heroes."

After stopping for ice cream sodas, Barbie drove back to the hotel. "I wonder if Ken and Steve are still sleeping," she said. As she parked the car, she saw two policemen dressed in blue coming off the walk. Mitch was between them—in handcuffs!

Kira leapt out of the car. She walked right up to Mitch. "How could you do a thing like that?" she demanded. "Especially you, who gets so much fun from this beach and this walk!"

Mitch smirked. "It was just a job. There are other beaches."

Barbie came up behind Kira. "Not if people like you ruin all the beaches."

"Excuse us, ladies," said one of the policemen. "We have to keep moving."

"By all means," said Kira, stepping aside.

Barbie put her arm around Kira's shoulders. "Good riddance to bad rubbish, as my grandma used to say."

Kira smiled. "Your grandma was a smart lady."

Christie and Teresa joined them. "The only bad part about all this is that the beach is still a mess," said Christie.

"The stuff they dumped last night will be washing up for days and days," Teresa added. "I hope it's not already too late."

They went back upstairs to Barbie and Christie's room. Right away, Barbie made a phone call.

"Who are you calling?" Teresa asked.

"Mayor Hanover," she replied. "I'm sure he knows what's happened, but I have something else I want to talk to him about."

The mayor went on and on with praise and thanks for all the gang had done. "There's still a problem, though," Barbie told him. "The beach is a wreck. I have an idea. Why doesn't the town have an all-out clean-up campaign? You could double your staff and get the beach back in shape."

"That's a great idea," Mayor Hanover said. "But we don't have the budget to hire more workers. You know how things are."

Barbie politely said good-bye. With a sigh, she plopped into a chair.

"No luck with the mayor?" asked Christie.

"He says he doesn't have enough money to hire a clean-up crew," Barbie said.

"What a shame," said Kira. "It was a good idea."

Barbie leaned forward in her chair. "I have another idea. If the mayor won't do anything, then we'll do it ourselves!"

9

The Crusade Is On

Barbie grabbed her straw hat from the table and started out the hotel room door.

The phone rang. It seemed to Barbie it had rung a million times in the past two days.

"Save the Beach headquarters," she answered.

"I saw one of your posters," said the woman on the other end. "Is it too late to sign up for a clean-up crew?"

"Not at all," Barbie assured her. "Just come on down."

Barbie hung up and hurried down to the beach. The past two days had been a whirlwind.

Barbie and the gang had put posters all over town asking people to help clean up the beach. The response had been great.

A local band said they would come down and play for all the workers. The local restaurants and stands donated free food for the clean-up crew. And Marv's Pizza Parlor offered to give all of his Friday earnings to the cause of keeping the beach clean. Since Friday was the day of his Rollerblade® in-line skate contest, it was sure to be a lot of money.

When she got to the walk, Barbie spotted Ken. "Look at all these people," he said. Up and down the beach, people wearing green ribbons were cleaning up. "And take a look at the water," he added.

Shielding her eyes against the bright sun, Barbie gazed at the ocean. Many boats of all kinds sat just offshore. People fished from the sides, but not for fish. They dragged large nets through the water, pulling up the floating garbage.

Christie came up the walk leading a clean-up group. She blew a whistle that hung on a string around her neck and told the group they could have a fifteen-minute break. "How is it going?" Barbie asked her.

"It's fun!" Christie answered. "I just passed Kira and her group. Kira was taking pictures of them all standing by their garbage bags. Steve has his group making up clean-beach rap songs as they work. And Teresa's group is now counting up all the dropped coins they've found. They have nearly forty dollars' worth to donate."

"Unbelievable," said Barbie.

"This band is super," Christie said, nodding toward the rock band playing nearby.

"I know," Barbie agreed. "I want to check on some of the other performers." Barbie started down the walk.

"Don't forget we're meeting at Marv's at five o'clock," Christie called her.

"How could I forget?" Barbie shouted back. "You remind me every time I see you."

Barbie had rounded up a small group of local

performers. She wanted this day to be fun as well as worthwhile.

She stood a moment and watched a clown entertain a group of children. He did a short skit in which a bunch of trick rubber flowers wilted each time his back was turned. The kids giggled as the clown tried silly ways to make the flowers stand straight. "If we turn our back on nature, this is what happens," he told the kids at the end.

Down the way were a mime and a juggler. Some puppeteers did a show about dolphins and the importance of keeping their water clean. And a local artist sketched free portraits of people wearing their green ribbons.

When she was sure everything was running smoothly, Barbie formed her own clean-up crew of people who were just arriving.

At a quarter to five, Barbie was working down on the beach with the others. The change was remarkable. The tide was bringing in nothing but clear, sparkling water.

"Are you ready?" asked Christie, running across the beach.

"Give me a minute to run upstairs," said Barbie. She handed her garbage bag to a fellow worker and ran up the beach.

In her room, she changed into her denim shorts with the star studs and red-white-and-blue design at the waist. She wore a hot pink midriff top and a denim vest. The gang had decided they'd all dress in their denim best for the show.

At exactly five, Barbie joined her friends in front of Marv's Pizza Parlor. Mayor Hanover himself was there making a speech. "You'd think this was all his idea," grumbled Christie.

"Oh, that's OK, as long as the job gets done?" said Barbie.

Soon Marv came out. He was a fat man wearing a long white apron. "Tonight is a big night," he told the large crowd. "Tonight we are working for a great cause. And we will have a new singles champ, thank goodness. That Mitch was getting on my nerves. At any rate, we will begin with a lovely new group, the Rockin' Rollers."

"Ready?" said Christie. She took a deep breath. "Here goes!"

10

Rolling Along

Barbie led the gang as they skated in a line to the center of the ring formed by the crowd. At first the music was soft. One by one, each of them put their heels together and began to spin.

Then the music kicked into a hard, driving beat. The friends linked arms and kicked their legs up high in front of them. Christie crouched low and rolled under their upraised legs. Then each of them did a special solo move.

When Barbie's turn came, she took a deep breath. She skated backward on one skate. Then she began to spin, still on one foot. The crowd cheered as she slowed to a stop.

After a few more moves, the routine ended. The crowd whistled and clapped as the friends bowed and skated off to the side. "We were great," said Christie, still breathless. "Barbie,

your spin was awesome!"

"Barbie, you were great," cried Kira.

"So were all of you," Barbie replied.

Just then, the next skaters came up. "Let's check out this group," said Teresa.

They stood and watched the skaters. Ken came up behind Barbie and rested his hand on her shoulder. "These guys are going to be hard to beat," Barbie said to him as she watched the skaters.

"No problem," Ken said.

There was something in Ken's eyes that made Barbie look twice. He seemed worried. "Is something wrong?" she asked.

"I can't hide anything from you," he said. He drew her aside. "I wasn't going to give you this until this evening. I didn't want to spoil the day for you if it was bad news. I know how much this means to you."

He handed her a letter. The return address said Worldwide Ballet School. "It arrived at your house yesterday. Skipper sent it to the hotel. The guy at the front desk asked me to give it to you."

Barbie's hands trembled as she held the letter. Two months ago she'd tried out for the ballet school. It was the most highly respected—and toughest—in the country. The school took only a handful of the best dancers each year. This letter would tell her if she'd been chosen or not.

"No sense waiting," she said. She tore open the envelope and read the letter. Then she looked up at Ken. She opened her mouth, but no words came out.

"Well?" Ken asked.

She clutched his arm. "I made it," she said softly. Then the news really hit her. "I did it! I made it!" she cried, hugging Ken tightly.

"What happened?" asked Kira. Christie and Teresa joined them.

"I'm going to the Worldwide Ballet School in September!" Barbie told them.

"All right!" cried Christie.

At that moment, Steve came over holding two large boot boxes. They told him Barbie's good news. "Way to go!" he said. "Is there anything you can't do?"

"Not anything I can think of," said Kira. "Hey, Steve, what's in the box?"

"Ken and I are tired of being left out," he said, handing a box to Ken. "So I ran to the sports store across the street and got each of us a brand new pair of Rollerblade® in-line skates."

The guys went to a bench and put on their skates. "Look at them," Teresa laughed. Ken and Steve clung to each other as they tried to get to their feet.

Christie skated over to Steve and ducked under his arm. Barbie took Ken's hand. "Barbie and I will have you guys skating in no time," said Christie.

When all the acts were finished, Marv called out the winners. "The winners of the group contest are the Rockin' Rollers! Your private pizza party awaits you whenever you want it," Marv said.

"Thank you, Marv!" cried Christie.

"And let's thank Marv for all the money he's giving to the Save the Beach Fund!" Barbie told the crowd. "The fund will be used to make sure the beach is kept clean and safe all year-round."

There was a loud cheer. Marv stood on a chair and held up his hands to silence the crowd. "The person we should really thank is Barbie. She gave us back our wonderful beach! Hurray for Barbie!"

"Hurray for Barbie!" the crowd yelled.

"Now everyone knows what we know," said Ken to Barbie. "You're the greatest."

Barbie smiled brightly. "Well, I have some pretty great friends, too."

"Hurray for Barbie!" the crowd cheered again.

Barbie waved to them. "Thanks!" She cried happily. "I'm just glad I could help!"